Musicians of Darfur

I0533451

Aman Charles

Musicians of Darfur
Aman Charles

Copyright © 2015 Aman Charles

Published by 1st World Publishing
P.O. Box 2211, Fairfield, Iowa 52556
tel: 641-209-5000 • fax: 866-440-5234
web: www.1stworldpublishing.com

First Edition
LCCN: 2015936454
ISBN: 978-1-4218-3732-1

Illustrations: Irene González Frizzera

Musicians of Darfur

By Aman Charles

(With a Little Help from My Friends)

CONTENTS

CHAPTER 1

Sometimes, luck can come to us at the worst of times.

It was the middle of August and terribly hot in the Darfur region of Sudan, Africa. Here lived two lucky brothers, Luis Carmono and Ulysses Delmar, who owned nothing whatsoever. Luis and Ulysses didn't have parents, but never once did they complain for more than what they had. They sang together happily every day, and at night, they slept peacefully looking forward to tomorrow.

Early one morning, rain began to fall gently on the brothers as they slept under the bright dessert sky. It almost never rains in Darfur and when it does it means one thing – good hunting! Luis and Ulysses grabbed their spears and were off. They tried to catch raindrops in their mouths while eagerly jogging toward a nearby river bed, but in a single moment, both boys stopped dead in their tracks. They heard something in the bushes, a magical sound, almost like a dream.

They started to aim their spears but realized the animal in the bushes wasn't moving. They approached cautiously. Luis moved the bushes aside with his spear, reached in and picked up the strangest object.

Ulysses thought it was a gun, but Luis said, "No, I think it is a music maker". They quickly hiked back to their hut where Luis washed it clean and studied its odd design. He plucked a string and it

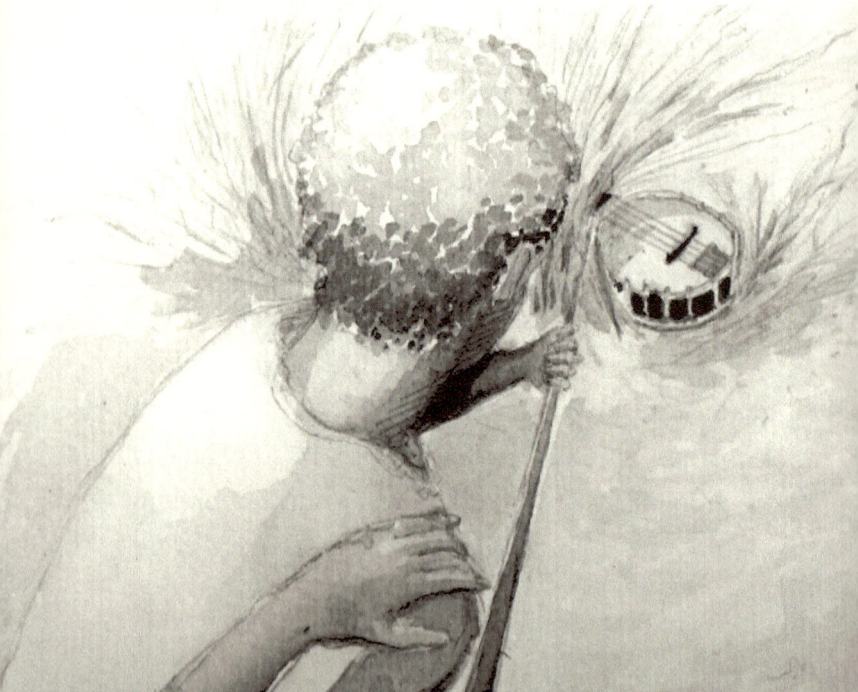

made a beautiful sound. The elegant high pitched sound was so relaxing they couldn't stop exploring its range. Day after day they plucked its strings, creating simple tunes and singing out stories they made up at the same moment. On the side of the music maker was written BANJO, so that's what they called it. BANJO. They played it for hours every day. The strange little instrument seemed almost magical. Just one simple song was all it took for the other villagers to love it too. Every night they would gather in a circle to listen to the new songs of the BANJO boys.

CHAPTER 2

Many months had passed and one morning while Luis and Ulysses were carrying water back from the river a helicopter appeared high in the sky over their heads. On the side was written POLICE in large letters. Both boys had the same thought … DANGER! They quickly gathered the villagers who watched the helicopter land. The police gathered everyone in a large group and the head officer spoke to them through a megaphone. "There is an army hiding nearby, waiting to attack the village"

The word "*attack*" made Luis's heart flutter. He could tell Ulysses was scared too. Everyone scattered like a game of tag when YOU'RE IT. I could hear Ulysses' heart pumping, stomach throbbing. Finally, after an hour of hiding away from our huts, we heard the police announce 'All clear!' and within minutes every officer was stuffed back into the helicopter and in a cloud of dust they were gone. The following day the police returned and told us that our village was no longer a safe place to live. They said that the people of the United Nations would protect us if we wanted to escape the war. They told us a plane would come for us and take us to a new home near London, England. They showed us many pictures of a city with tall buildings. The police told us that the choice was ours, but we had to decide quickly.

That afternoon Ulysses and I decided we would go to London. For one hour we jumped and jumped and jumped with happiness, singing all the while. We packed our banjo in our sleeping blanket and waited and waited and waited. I was so happy, I thought I might faint.

Finally the waiting ended. There was growing commotion everywhere. Everyone was jumping, higher and higher with excitement when a huge red and grey plane landed in the dessert a quarter mile from our village.

Everyone waved and yelled. I looked toward the sun, slowly setting, and said a little thank you prayer.

Six hours later, in the middle of the night, the plane was loaded …but we weren't on it. A large white soldier in a tan colored uniform told the rest of the village they would have to wait for another plane the following day. By this time the moon was high in the sky and Ulysses and I, exhausted with excitement, went back to our hut to sleep.

Ulysses mumbled something as he was getting ready for bed, but I couldn't hear it and I couldn't sleep. I wanted to stay up and wait for the new plane to arrive. I looked outside. The sky was so beautiful. I wondered if the sky would be so beautiful in London. I waited and waited. No plane. Finally, I was so weary; I got into bed and fell asleep.

The next morning I woke up to the smell of my favorite breakfast, fresh squirrel cooked on the leaf of the Citrullus Colocyn cactus.

I went to wake Ulysses when I realized he wasn't there. He must have woken up before me. I quickly got up, stepped outside the hut, and for a moment

my breath stopped. Before me was an airplane four times larger than the one last night. It looked like a metal bird, the size of a mountain, sitting smack in the middle of our village. It was shinier than anything I had ever seen. I spied the pilot, whose bright smile, gentle eyes and soft brown skin made him look like a noble prince, who at the moment was answering questions (mostly from Ulysses).

He was talking loudly and told everyone to take only what they needed and to begin loading cargo on the plane immediately. I gathered my blankets, my lucky spear, and of course, our banjo. A moment later, I walked onto the plane.

Again, I almost stopped my breath. Never had I seen anything so clean and shiny and full of gadgets and multicolored lights. I was scared, excited and happier than I had ever been, all at the same time.

We put our blankets and gear in small compartments near the front of the plane. Another soldier helped us strap into our seats and the pilot announced his name was Captain Edward. Our great journey was about to begin!

Captain Edward announced that he was turning up the engines and not to be afraid of the noise or the shaking. This was natural, he said. We were all excited and nervous, but when the plane lifted off the ground we weren't afraid at all. We were too

busy looking at brightly colored pictures of our new home near London and fighting to stare out the window at the dessert below. One of the villagers started singing and soon we were all signing. The ride was calm and smooth and after two hours, almost everyone fell asleep. I fell into a deep sleep and dreamt about our new home.

CHAPTER 3

It was nothing like our village home. Our new home had a soft bed to sleep on, a television with color, and it even had a cold-box to store our food! We didn't have to hunt anymore the way we used to. Our new home was surrounded by buildings stocked with all the food we would ever need.

When I woke up from my dream to the sound of cheering, I looked out the window and found that we had almost arrived. The captain announced that the plane would be slowing down to get ready to land and I felt a flutter in my stomach. The airport was filled with planes and helicopters. At last, we landed. We all helped each other with the little luggage we had and another loud announcement instructed us to wait for a bus that would soon arrive and take us to our new home.

We waited near the giant airplane, just standing there, but the bus hadn't come. There was a bad smell in the air. I looked at the sun, it was mid afternoon. In a moment the wait was over. A huge two-story bus rounded a corner and stopped right in front of Ulyseus and myself.

"All aboard!" said the driver.

We picked up our sacks and got on.

Ulysses and I got to sit in seats on the top of the bus in the open air. It was remarkable! Massive buildings loomed before us and people were scattered everywhere as they frantically moved from one building to the next. I took a deep breath and smiled. The air was filled with the scent of foods I had never eaten before and everywhere cars honked like angry birds. The sites we saw were fantastic. It was like living in a jungle of manmade mountains.

Before I knew it I saw a sign which read: *Welcome to London!* We were in London? Already? The bus driver was well-versed in the city's history and excitedly shared tidbits of information with us as we drove up and down the winding streets. He explained how London is the biggest city in Britain and how it was the first city in the world to have an underground railroad. I didn't understand the full importance of these facts, but I was excited about them none the less.

Finally we arrived at our new London home.

It was big, tall and beautiful! It was a high-rise

building that had hundreds of windows and looked just like the pictures we had seen on the plane. I couldn't wait to get inside and have a proper new home.

We all gathered into a large, brightly lit room where we were greeted by the Housing Counselor. I was so mesmerized by the smooth, glassy surface of the floor and winding staircases that I almost didn't hear him as he handed us our special key cards and told us about the rooms he had assigned to us. Each card had a room number on it and we were told to carry our card whenever we left our room. If we needed help, the key would be needed to help identify us. The councilor also told us to carry our cards whenever we came for mealtime. All of the councilors already knew we were the villagers from Darfur.

I looked at the number on our key. It was 735. We must be close to the top floor. The Housing Councilor told us his name was Arthur and that he was in room 848 if we needed his help.

He directed us to an elevator, which is a small room that lifts people up and down a building. It has a shiny door that opens automatically when you push a button that lights up like a flashlight.

Arthur escorted us all the way to our room where he handed us another card. He said it was a food card and we would need it to receive our meals.

To me it looked like a rectangular piece of plastic. Ulysses and I looked at it with curiosity.

Just then, I felt dizzy. My mouth grew dry and my head felt heavy. A few moments later, blackness seemed to dominate light as I fainted.

When I woke up, I found myself lying on a bed, as soft as sheep's wool, and cleaner than anything I had ever seen in Darfur. This was our new home.

"What happened?" I said.

"You fainted" said Arthur, "the trip must have been a lot for you." I had a glass of water and felt better. Ulysses and I said good-bye and thank you to Arthur and started to unpack our few belongings.

Once we were through, I picked up the banjo and started to play. Ulysses joined in and we made up songs just as we did in Darfur. But this time the unique sound of the music was inspired by a new vibrant rhythm.

CHAPTER 4

The next day was bright and sunny, but cooler than what I was used to. Ulysses and I spent hours inspecting every corner of our new home and finally decided to venture out on the busy, people-filled streets of London.

We found a spot in the shade near a small brick wall by a cobblestone road. We put down our blanket and sat on the sidewalk as pale skinned, well dress people passed us by with unfavorable glances. The air smells so much different here than it did in our old home. In Darfur, the air smelled clean and dry, but here it smells old and dirty and wet.

"Let's sing" I said to Ulysses. He nodded back approvingly and unwrapped the blanket that protected our music maker. Ulysses played first, quietly, but skillfully with a soft, mysterious lilt. The music seemed to just flow from his fingers.

Strangers on the road would stop and smile when they saw the scene. Soon it was my turn. The banjo felt alive under my touch. I closed my eyes and began to play my song. I sang with it, spontaneously, involuntarily, with no effort at all. Nothing existed but me and the melody that whirled almost automatically from my hands.

When I opened my eyes, I saw a small crowd that had formed around me and my grinning brother. They began to applaud us. They asked if we were part of a band. They wanted to know everything about us. Many of them even put money on our blanket. Ulysses said, "White skinned people have too much money", but they all assured us it was money well spent and some of them asked us to perform at public gatherings.

Almost every day we sang on the sidewalk and whenever we did our music brought smiles to the blank, lonely faces of the pale skinned Londoners.

Every day the crowds grew larger. People snapped photos of us and told other people, who told other people, and before long, people started bringing chairs and blankets and were waiting for us to arrive. Some of them stayed for hours. It became a routine. Every morning, my brother and I would take turns playing our banjo in the shade of our tree and when it rained, someone would always cover us with umbrellas.

Day after day more people would gather and listen to our music. It became a street party. Arthur had some of our Darfur villagers selling balloons and homemade candies and even whole meals with African sweet-water. Every day we would see new faces. Every day we made more friends and learned new names. Many people invited us to sing at libraries or restaurants or outdoor stages in the park.

Once someone showed us our picture in a newspaper and told us we were on TV as well.

"I've never heard anything quite like it." "It's different every time!" "How did they learn to play like that?" People said.

CHAPTER 5

Everyone was talking about us with so much excitement, but we were just simple villagers from Darfur. Making music made us happy and we were happier still knowing that it made others happy as well.

People began recording our music and taking more photos and making movies, but we never noticed much. We played for the joy it gave us and the joy it spread around.

One special sunny day Arthur brought some new people to talk to us. He said they were from Albert Hall in London.

He told us they wanted us to sing and play on a stage rather than a sidewalk. He said Albert Hall could hold thousands and thousands of people.

CHAPTER 6

Suddenly it seemed our small, local street concert
was to be relocated to Albert Hall …in three weeks!
I could hardly believe it! Ulysses didn't actually
believe it, not until a week later when Arthur took
us on a tour and showed us the stage we would be
playing on.

Excitement was everywhere. When we turned on the TV, we heard people talking about THE BANJO BOYS from Darfur. When we switched on the radio, we heard ourselves singing.

Every day we continued to play on the streets. Every day more and more people came to hear us and learn more about Darfur, our home. When Ulysses sang, I played the Banjo and when I sang, Ulysses played the banjo. We enjoyed every moment.

Time passes quickly when you're doing what you love to do and before we knew it, it was concert day. We felt as if we had just left our village life in Darfur and now, here we were on stage at Albert Hall.

CHAPTER 7

Arthur led us out on stage. It was dark, but we could hear the rumbles and echoes of thousands of people.

Suddenly a loud voice announce, "Ladies and gentlemen! No introduction is required! I give you the musical genius of THE BANJO BOYS of Darfur!

"Give it up for the B-Boys!"

We stepped out to the edge of the stage, simply with two stools and our banjo. The lights were bright and hot and we had never seen so many people gathered in one place before. Everyone was so clean and well dressed. The throng of people sat in rows farther than we could see, but we saw many old familiar faces from the street sitting near the front rows. Everyone was clapping.

I smiled at Ulysses, and we began to play. The clapping died down, and the only sound we heard was the song dancing through our veins. It was an awe-inspiring experience, playing with my brother on a stage and both Ulysses and I realized we had never played like this before. Something new was happening. I felt elevated, calm and silent as if the music was playing *me*. We couldn't stop and at times burst into laughter or tears at exactly the same time.

It brought us so much joy Ulysses actually howled with delight. When the song concluded, sixty eight minutes later, the crowd jumped to their feet applauding so loud Ulysses and I covered our ears out of fear. Some people even whistled.

The performance was over and people slowly left the giant hall. Arthur drove us back home and no one spoke a word. Even too much happiness can leave you exhausted. I went straight to bed, my head still spinning with the delightful events of the night.

CHAPTER 8

The following morning was rainy and grey, which is common in London. Arthur, with his usual mischievous grin, brought us a newspaper and we were stunned to find Our picture was on the front page! It read:

THE BANJO BOYS
Musicians of Darfur

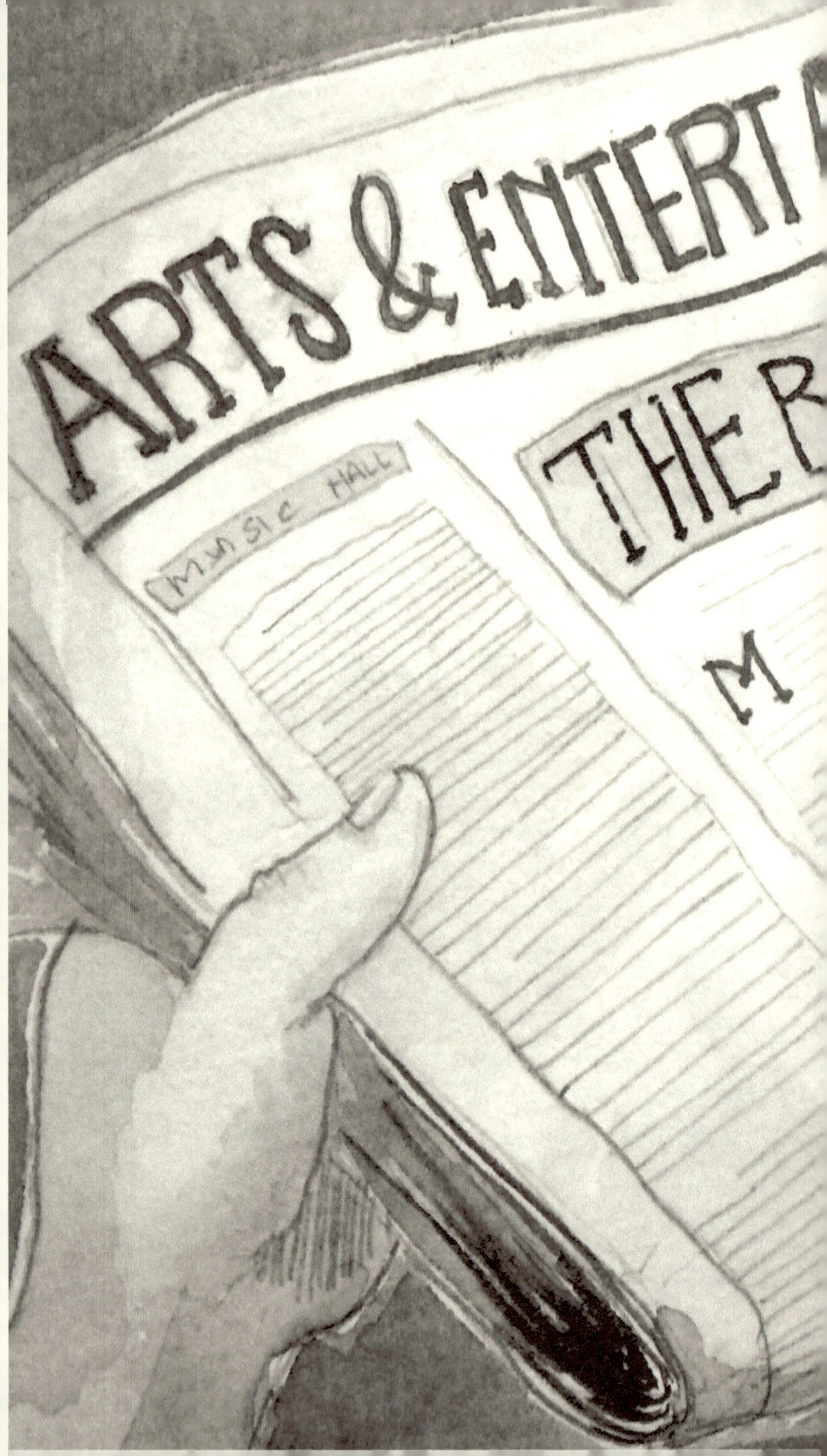
ARTS & ENTERT
MUSIC HALL
THE R
M

I smiled from ear to ear and both Ulysses and I jumped like baby rabbits.

Arthur had told us that during last night's recital he overheard the men from Albert Hall trying to reorganize their schedule to fit in more BANJO BOYS performances.

He also said, "Boys, we have to start talking about money".

Last night Albert Hall collected over four hundred thousand dollars in ticket sales. They also collected one hundred and eight thousand dollars in donations for the HELP SUDAN FUND. He said The HELP SUDAN FUND was founded by the LOST BOYS OF SUDAN. Their goal is to bring food and water to children in Darfur and to build schools to educate the uneducated.

Ulysses laughed unrestrained and choked out, "If we buy banjos for every villager in Darfur it would be the richest country in the world and they could send money to London to help clean up the air!"

I blurted out, "How much money will it take to build schools in Darfur? How many more concerts can we set up? People must enjoy our music as much as we do, how can we play for them all!"

Arthur had a friendly grin on his face because he already knew what needed to be done. "Boys," he said, we are going to record all your performances to raise money for Darfur. Last night's performance was uploaded to YouTube and has already received thirteen million hits. The Banjo boys are going viral".

Some of our village people brought breakfast to our room, and we talked about new songs we could perform and what we should call the first new album. Everyone agreed the title should be **The Way We Work.**

CHAPTER 9

Arthur organized everything. He handled all the paper work and money matters and found a music studio who agreed to record our daily performances on the street.

We made great progress and every day we saw new newspapers and magazines filled with our photos.

Arthur said money was pouring into the Help Sudan Fund and that it was only going to grow.

And he was right. One day, just after finishing lunch, Arthur handed me the phone.

When I hung up, I was debating if we should do it. Ulysses asked, "Do what? Teach banjo lessons to the queen?"

"No silly. Appear in a national TV interview

Ulysses said it sounded like a great idea, but teaching banjo lessons at Buckingham Palace would be more fun.

Arthur agreed, it was a great idea and arranged a meeting at 4:30 PM. That was the first of many TV interviews to come.

The TV studio was located at Trafalgar Square in the center of London. When we met Emily Green the interview lady, I began to get nervous. What if she asks difficult questions? But it never happened. She asked us some simple questions and it didn't matter that we didn't understand all the words. Then she told us she had a surprise for us. She asked if we would perform right now in the TV station.

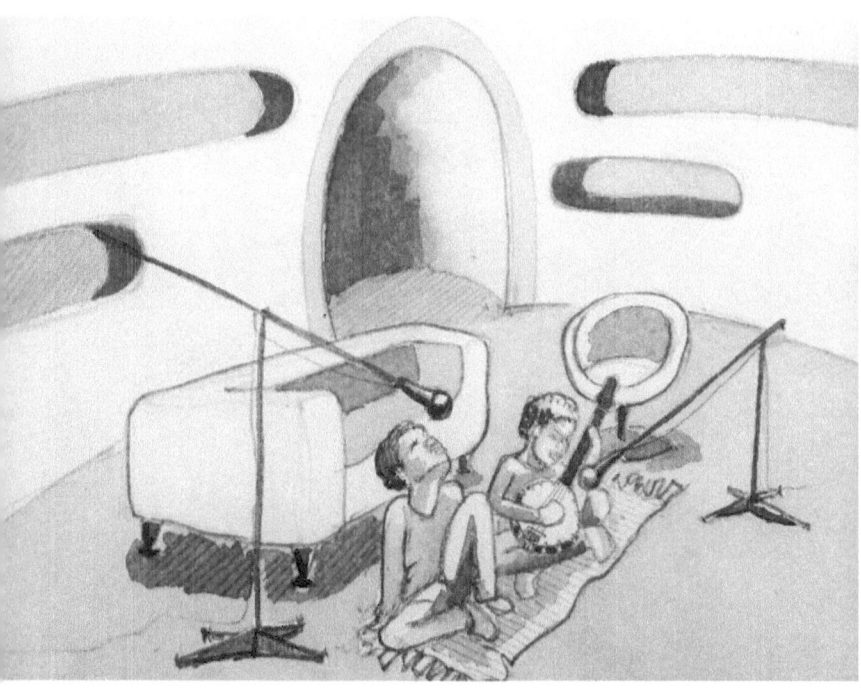

She promised that the concert would be broadcast world-wide. Ulysses and I were always eager to perform. We were better at singing than speaking anyway. Arthur and Emily Green arranged some microphones and spread out a blanket on the floor and after a moment of silence Ulysses started to sing just as I pulled the first string on the banjo.

CHAPTER 10

Three weeks later, Ulysses and I were eating breakfast when Author showed up to join us. He proudly announced that the Help Sudan Fund had raised over nine million dollars and told us over 80,000 seats were sold out at our next concert in the new Olympic Stadium in London's Stratford district.

CHAPTER 11

It was a busy three weeks and today was concert
day. I asked Arthur if we could go to an open field
and just relax for a while, maybe play some games.
"That's a great idea!" he said and arranged for a ride
to Hyde Park in Central London. We walked and
talked the whole time and Ulysses kept us laughing.
Three hours passed very quickly and Arthur
reminded us that it was time to leave for Olympic
Stadium. We arrived shortly before six o'clock and
after forty minutes of rest Arthur escorted us onto
the performance stage.

Everyone was clapping as we spread out our
blanket and the sound was almost deafening.

A few minutes later I heard the music flowing through me as it always did.

We played for more than an hour. I felt elevated, my heart overstuffed with happiness and tears in my eyes. Then gently, like a puff of baby's breath, I breathed out and listened as my heart slowly stopped pumping …in perfect rhythm with the end of our song.

So that's my story. Often I wonder about who lost that wonderful banjo in the bushes of Darfur. And of course, I watch over Ulysses and I think to myself, what a wonderful world

Aman Charles writes books, makes music, plays soccer and disc golf, and rides his mountain bike on the trails of Southeast Iowa.

Contact: 1stworldlibrary@gmail.com

Irene González Frizzera started drawing and painting at an early age and never stopped. She graduated from Escuela Universitaria Centro de Diseño (University of Industrial Design in Montevideo) with a degree in Textile Design. See her online portfolio at: www.behance.net/Irene_ene

Proceeds from the sale of this book are sent to:

The HELP SUDAN FUND founded by the LOST BOYS OF SUDAN whose goal is to provide food and water to children in Darfur and to build schools to educate the uneducated.

Programs include recruiting school administration, integrating community involvement, providing funding to teachers and administrators, constructing school buildings, and drilling water wells for the school campus.